This edition published by Parragon Books Ltd in 2014

Parragon Books Ltd
Chartist House
15–17 Trim Street
Bath BA1 1HA, UK
www.parragon.com

ISBN 978-1-4723-5652-9

Printed in China

Mama Hook Knows Best

A Pirate Parent's Favourite Fables

Written by
Sharon Osbourne

Illustrated by
Massimiliano Narciso
and the
Disney Storybook Artists

Bath • New York • Cologne • Melbourne • Delhi
Hong Kong • Shenzhen • Singapore • Amsterdam

Hello, popinjays! It is I, Mama Hook. Surely you've heard of me. In my day, I was the bravest, most beloved pirate ever to sail the Never Sea!

I've battled sea monsters ...

I've hunted for priceless treasure ...

and, most daring of all, I raised my son ...

James Bartholomew Hook, a great and glorious pirate captain —

mostly.

Over the years, I've gathered some stories and used them

as a way to teach my son all about the

legendary pirate code.

These swashbuckling tales delighted my little James

and taught him a lesson or two – I hope.

Would you care to read some of them with me? Splendid! Let's begin with ...

THE GREAT SHIP RACE

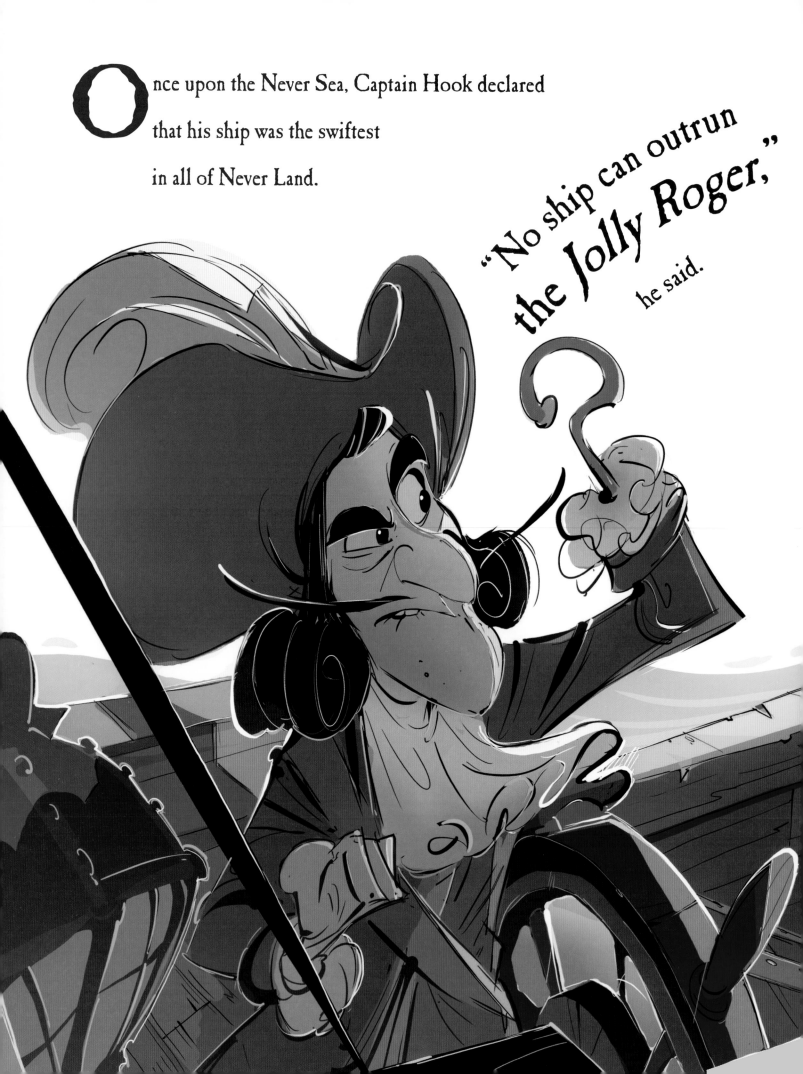

Once upon the Never Sea, Captain Hook declared that his ship was the swiftest in all of Never Land.

"No ship can outrun the Jolly Roger," he said.

"Yo-ho!" cried Jake. "Let Bucky give it a go!"

Captain Hook was outraged. "Bucky? Why, that barnacle boat is slower than a turtle."

There was only one thing to do ... RACE!

The first ship to shore would win.

Ready,
steady,
go!

Bucky shot through the water, setting sail on a steady course.

"Yay-hey, straight away!" shouted Jake.

But Captain Hook was so sure he would win, he wasn't
in a hurry at all.

"Smee! My tea."

The *Jolly Roger* stood still in the water as
Bucky sailed closer to shore.

"Uh, Cap'n? Shouldn't we be setting sail?"

"**Stop worrying**, Smee! We'll sail after me nap. Now where is Captain Cuddly?"

When Captain Hook woke up he was shocked to see that Bucky was nearly at the finish line!

"What are you waiting for, you scallywag?

Those pipsqueak pirates are about to win! Full speed ahead!"

"Aye, aye, Cap'n."

FINISH

They pulled up the anchor to
try to catch Bucky ...

but it was too late.

Jake's swift and steady ship had won the race.
And as for Captain Hook, all he got was a visit
from the Tick Tock Croc.

Did you catch the lesson there, dearies?

MAMA HOOK'S
GOLDEN RULE

NEVER LAND PIRATES
ALWAYS SAIL A STEADY
COURSE AND PAY
ATTENTION TO THEIR
PIRATE DUTIES.

Now, one thing James loves most in the world – besides his mummy – is treasure. He can never get enough of it!
But, sometimes, too much of a good thing can be bad.

You'll see what I mean in our next story ...

THE PIRATES AND THEIR REFLECTIONS

Once upon the Rainbow River, Captain Hook and Mr Smee were carrying a **payload of plunder.**

Not to worry, popinjays.

That means they had a lot of treasure.

As Captain Hook neared the river
he spotted another pirate.
This pirate had his hands full
of treasure, too!

"Look, Smee,
that handsome
buccaneer has

more booty than
he can carry."

Smee looked, but he didn't see a thing.

That's because it was all pish posh! Captain Hook
thought he'd seen another pirate – but he was looking
at his **own reflection in the water.**

The greedy captain wanted all the treasure for himself.
"On the count of three, we'll jump out and grab the
treasure from that clueless bilge rat.

One,

two,

three!"

Splash!

Captain Hook and Mr Smee fell right into the Rainbow River!

"Cap'n? Maybe it's time to get your eyes checked?"

All the captain's treasure floated away.

"Save me treasure, Smee!"

Tick tock!
Tick tock!

"Never mind the treasure, Smee! **Save me!**"

So the lesson to be learned from that tale ...

MAMA HOOK'S
GOLDEN RULE

GOOD PIRATES AREN'T
GREEDY AND THEY NEVER
TAKE THINGS THAT DON'T
BELONG TO THEM

I'm afraid that's a lesson
James never did learn.

Ah, now this last story is my absolute favourite, my little buccaneers. James never did care for it, though. I'm not sure why.

THE PIRATE WHO
CRIED CROC

Once upon Shipwreck Beach,
Captain Hook was up to no good.

He was stealing other people's treasure.

Whenever the scoundrel spotted someone
with treasure, he would yell,

"Oh, save me from the **crocodile!**"

And when the dear, sweet pirates would rush off to help,

Captain Hook's crew would nab their treasure. Oh, my!

"Oh, save me from the crocodile!"

This went on ...

day ...   after day ...   after day ...

until Captain Hook had stolen **all** the riches in Never Land!

Then one day ... **tick tock, tick tock** ...
the **real croc** came to Never Land.
But when Captain Hook cried,

"Save me from the crocodile!"

no one believed him.

"That scallywag's just after our treasure."

"Save me from the crocodile!"

But Captain Hook wasn't trying to steal any treasure that day. He was too busy ... running from a certain croc! TICK TOCK.

So that story proves ...

MAMA HOOK'S
GOLDEN RULE

A NEVER LAND PIRATE
NEVER TELLS A LIE.

Even though James can be a bit naughty at times,
I'm so proud of my little pirate.

But one thing I'll never understand is how anyone could be afraid of an itty-bitty, little crocodile. Oh, I think I hear James calling.

"Ayeeeee! Save me, Mummy!"

Till next time, popinjays.

"Mummy's coming, dearest!"